DICKY-DUCK

Written and illustrated by David W[right]

Book 6: The Duckling Race

For Jed Grant, who helped Dicky-Duck to take off

Also available in this series:

Book 1: The Hatching

Book 2: Dicky-Duck and the Mink

Book 3: Dicky-Duck Explores

Book 4: Sports Day

Book 5: Dicky-Duck and the Kite

In late Spring each year, there is a very special competition held for all of the baby ducklings who have not yet grown their adult feathers. It is called the Duckling Race, and Dicky-Duck very much wanted to win.

For as many years as any duck could remember, the race had been won by one of the big ducklings from the reservoir, and he thought it was about time that somebody else had a turn.

Dicky-Duck trained three times a day, and his training diet was - you've guessed it - baked bean sandwiches!

Quite a few of the wild ducklings who visited the pond at Windrush Cottage were also keen to race, and Dicky-Duck persuaded them to team up with him so they could help each other.

He introduced them to his special training diet. This made quite a change from water beetles and pond weed and they grew bigger and stronger at a remarkable rate.

They decided to call themselves the 'Windy Ducks' as they came from Windrush Cottage, which in view of their diet was really quite appropriate!

Every day the ducklings worked so hard to get fit. They ran around the lawn ten times a day (which is an extremely long way for a duckling), did stretching exercises, had baked bean sandwich eating contests and practised sprinting across the pond.

It was an incredible sight to see a line of ducklings pelting across the surface of the water like miniature jet skis!

They got faster each day until they had to find a bigger stretch of water because they couldn't stop in time to avoid crashing into the bank!

When the day of the race finally came, the 'Windy Ducks' could hardly wait to get started. They had eaten the most enormous plate of baked bean sandwiches for breakfast. You could have said that they were 'full of beans', which of course they were!

Sue had given them each a red hairband to wear around their necks so that they all looked part of the same team. They all felt very proud of themselves.

It would soon be time to go to the lake where the race was to be held, and they hopped from webbed foot to webbed foot with excitement.

The race took place on a large mill pond not far from Windrush Cottage. Along one end of the pond was a long straight bank which acted as a dam - but also provided a very convenient starting and finishing line.

As the ducklings arrived from all over the county, they jostled for good places along the dam and waited expectantly for the starting quack.

All they had to do then was to race up to the other end of the lake, go around a small island, then race all the way back to the dam. There were no other rules - the first to reach the dam was the winner.

The reservoir ducklings had already claimed the best place in the middle of the dam, so Dicky-Duck led his team over to the far side where they were less likely to get trampled on in the rush.

They got a few warning stares from some of the bigger ducklings as if to say, "Keep out of our way!" Dicky-Duck told his team to ignore them and they picked out a good spot in the shade near the bank.

The big fat starting drake waddled importantly up to a tree stump and scrambled up so that all the ducklings could hear his quack. The race would soon be started!

After what seemed to be an endless wait, the starting drake finally made sure that all the ducklings were in position. He took in a great lungful of air and stretched his neck as high as he could. He opened his beak and every duckling quivered on its toes, ready to leap into action.

'QUAAAAAACK!' went the starting drake, and chaos broke out as nearly a hundred brown balls of fluff churned up the lake into a flurry of spray!

The 'Windy Ducks' got a good start, and they chased after the front runners - who turned out to be the reservoir ducklings.

Although the reservoir ducklings were whizzing across the lake at an alarming rate, Dicky-Duck's training started to pay off as the 'Windy Ducks' began to close the gap. As they approached the island at the far end of the lake, the plucky team had drawn level - much to the dismay of the leaders.

Then, just as Dicky-Duck squeezed into the inside lane to try and find a way through, three of the reservoir ducklings deliberately slowed down and blocked his path.

The only way through was around the outside, which would give the leading group a chance to get even further ahead.

However, the 'Windy Ducks' were not to be beaten so easily, and as one they dived beak-first at the ducklings who were in their way and pecked their bottoms hard! The big ducklings shot into the air with surprise, and the 'Windy Ducks' immediately darted underneath them.

The leading ducklings had gained a few seconds, but Dicky-Duck felt sure they could catch them up if they tried.

"Up a gear Windys!" shouted Dicky-Duck, and the gallant team launched themselves forward in a last desperate attempt to snatch the lead.

The finishing line was now within sight, and the 'Windy Ducks' were right on the tails of the leaders. But every time they tried to get past, the bigger ducklings swerved to block their way.

On Dicky-Duck's signal, the 'Windy Ducks' split up and tried to go around on both sides at once. Confused by this sudden change of tactics, the bigger ducklings hesitated, allowing the 'Windy Ducks' to draw level!

The bigger ducklings began pecking viciously at the 'Windy Ducks' to hold them back, whilst one of them forged ahead on his own.

Dicky-Duck wasn't going to give up now, and twisting away from the grasp of the duckling blocking his way, he made a final desperate dash for the line.

Calling on his last reserves of strength, he shot forward until he was neck and neck with the leading duckling. There were only three metres to the line, but the reservoir duckling's superior size began to tell as he gradually drew ahead of Dicky-Duck once again!

But just when Dicky-Duck thought that all was lost, it was his training diet that finally made the difference!

The baked bean sandwiches he had eaten earlier suddenly exploded into action with such force that Dicky-Duck was blasted across the line first - to everyone's total amazement!

The amazement turned to dismay as the fumes wafted over the spectating ducks, but fortunately the breeze soon cleared them away!

When Dicky-Duck was asked to step up and collect the winner's medal, he called over the rest of the 'Windy Ducks' to join him.

"It was a team effort," he said, "and we must all share the medal!" He stretched the ribbon so they could all wear it together for the winner's photo!

Dicky's Duck-tionary!

Here are some of the more difficult words to be found in this book:

appropriate	*proper, suitable*	**introduced**	*brought into use*
chaos	*disorder, confusion*	**jostled**	*pushed, bumped*
churned	*stirred up*	**launched**	*went into action*
confused	*mixed up*	**miniature**	*very small*
convenient	*handy, useful*	**pelting**	*running very fast*
deliberately	*on purpose*	**persuaded**	*talked into, convinced*
dismay	*alarm*	**plucky**	*brave*
expectantly	*in suspense*	**quivered**	*shook, trembled*
flurry	*swirling cloud*	**remarkable**	*unusual*
forged	*moved ahead*	**reservoir**	*large man-made lake*
gallant	*bold, daring*	**superior**	*greater*
ignore	*take no notice*	**tactics**	*plans*
incredible	*hard to believe*	**wafted**	*drifted gently*

EDUCATIONAL NOTE

The hilarious Dicky-Duck series of children's books is loved by all children of Primary School age and the challenging vocabulary is ideally suited for National Curriculum Key Stages 1 and 2 (see Dicky's Duck-tionary!). Being both funny and highly motivational, they are particularly valuable for children beginning to read independently or simply to have read to them for fun.

Children especially love the pictures, which encourage lots of stimulating discussion. Parents and carers alike will enjoy sharing many aspects of these immensely popular stories. Humour is now recognised as one of the most significant boosts to learning - especially reading - and Dicky-Duck provides a powerful and stress free way to encourage reading development.

Further information about this series can be found on Dicky-Duck's 'Webbed Foot' site on **www.mwmsites.com/dickyduck**

Alternatively, you can contact LTL Publishing by telephone **(01460) 64752**, Fax **(01460) 65957** or E-mail **davidwright@ltlpublishing.freeserve.co.uk**

About the Author....

David Wright started telling Dicky-Duck stories to his two young children at bedtime, and realised that by far the most successful were those which made them laugh. Encouraged by their enthusiasm, he began to write down the best ones and illustrated them as a hobby.

When David's wife read the books to children of all ages at local Primary schools where she was teaching, their response was incredible. Even the naughtiest children were captivated by the stories and pictures, and you could hear a pin drop in the classroom whenever they were read!

Constant demand from children who wanted to buy the books convinced David it was worthwhile getting them published. This is the result, which is dedicated to all those children with grateful thanks for their positive and enthusiastic support.